# Little Grey Rabbit's Birthday

## Alison Uttley
### pictures by Margaret Tempest

GALLERY BOOKS
An Imprint of W. H. Smith Publishers Inc.
112 Madison Avenue
New York City 10016

First published in the United States by Gallery Books,
an imprint of W.H. Smith Publishers Inc.,
112 Madison Avenue, New York, New York 10016.

First published 1944.
Text copyright © The Alison Uttley Literary Property Trust 1986.
Illustrations copyright © The Estate of Margaret Tempest 1986.
This arrangement © William Collins Sons & Co Ltd 1990.
Produced for Gallery Books by Joshua Morris Publishing, Inc.
in association with William Collins Sons & Co Ltd.
All rights reserved.
Decorated capital by Mary Cooper.
Alison Uttley's original story has been abridged for this book.
ISBN 0-8317-5627-6
**Printed in Great Britain**

Gallery Books are available for bulk purchase for sales
promotions and premium use. For details write or telephone
the Manager of Special Sales, W.H. Smith Publishers, Inc.,
112 Madison Avenue, New York, New York 10016. (212) 532-6600

# FOREWORD

Of course you must understand that Grey Rabbit's home had no electric light or gas. The candles were made from the pith of rushes dipped in wax from the wild bees' nests, which Squirrel found. Water there was in plenty, but it did not come from a faucet. It flowed from a spring outside, which rose up from the ground and went to a brook. Grey Rabbit cooked on a wood fire for there was no coal in that part of the country. Tea did not come from India, but from a little herb known very well to country people, who once dried it and used it in their cottage homes. Bread was baked from wheat ears, which Hare and Grey Rabbit gleaned in the cornfields.

The doormats were braided rushes, like country-made mats, and cushions were stuffed with wool gathered from the hedges where sheep had pushed through the thorns. As for the looking-glass, Grey Rabbit found the glass, dropped from a lady's handbag, and Mole made a frame for it. Usually the animals gazed at themselves in the still pools as so many country children have done. The country ways of Grey Rabbit were the country ways known to the author.

**S**quirrel and Hare were gardening one fine day. Squirrel was sowing dandelions and Hare was watering them.

"It's little Grey Rabbit's birthday on Midsummer Day," said Squirrel, as she shook the dandelion heads and let the seeds fly.

"I think it's time for my birthday," pondered Hare. "It's weeks and weeks since I had a birthday."

"It isn't your turn, Hare. Grey Rabbit hasn't had a birthday for a whole year. We must give her a nice present."

"Of course," agreed Hare. "A cake or something. Yes, something we can all share."

"Yes. A birthday cake with candles on it," said Squirrel.

"I don't like the taste of candles," objected Hare.

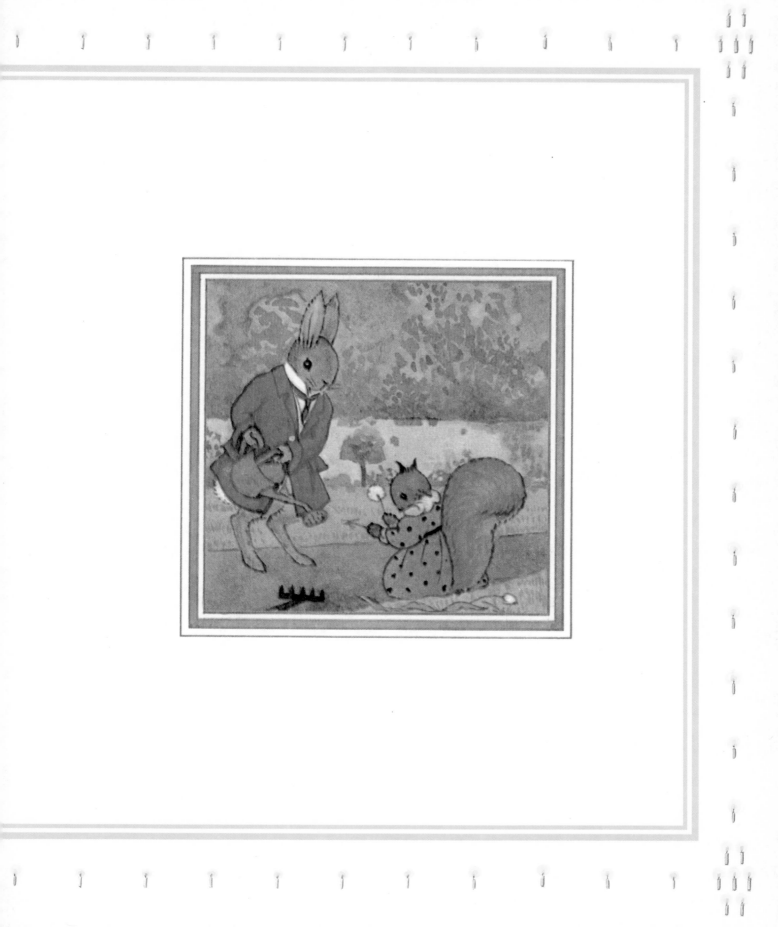

"They're not to eat!" cried Squirrel. "They are to show how old you are. Three candles if you are three years old."

"And a hundred if you are a hundred years old," said Hare. "Oh, Squirrel, can we make the cake ourselves?"

"I think so," nodded Squirrel. "We can't ask Grey Rabbit to make it. It must be a secret."

Just then Grey Rabbit came running out of the house.

"Oh Squirrel!" she cried. "I asked you to sow lettuce seeds and you are putting dandelions in the garden. Another gardener will sow them for us."

"Who's that?" asked Squirrel.

"The wind," said Grey Rabbit. "He'll plant dandelion seeds."

"Grey Rabbit!" interrupted Hare. "Squirrel and I have been saying that your b-b-- that it will be your b-b--"

"Shh! Not a word!" whispered Squirrel.

"No! Not a word! It's a secret," said Hare hastily.

"A secret from me?" asked Grey Rabbit.

"We can't tell you. It wouldn't be a secret if you knew," explained Squirrel.

"No, we can't speak it. It's something that mustn't be told," added Hare with importance. But the secret was just about to hop out of Hare's mouth, when Squirrel rushed at him with a handkerchief and tied him up.

"Have you got a toothache?" asked Grey Rabbit.

Hare shook his head, but not a word could he utter.

"Will you come for a walk to visit the Speckledy Hen?" asked Grey Rabbit. "I want to get some eggs."

"We'll come, won't we, Hare?" said Squirrel, throwing down the rake.

"Mum-mum-mum-m-m" grunted Hare.

They went through the field where Moldy Warp lived.

Moldy Warp was sitting in his house, smoking his pipe. "Hello!" he cried when the three friends arrived. "This is a surprise."

He hurried to fetch glasses of heather ale, and
brought them outside.

"Oh dear! Have you got a toothache, Hare?" he
asked.

"No, he's keeping a secret," explained Squirrel.

Hare looked at the heather ale and he looked at
Squirrel, till Mole took pity on him and untied the
knot.

"I'm going to tell," he exclaimed. "I can't keep it in. I shall burst if I don't tell somebody."

"No! No!" cried Squirrel, shaking his arm.

"Come inside, and whisper to me and the door," said Mole kindly. Hare followed him into the passage.

"It's Grey Rabbit's birthday on Midsummer Day, and we are going to make a cake," he said breathlessly.

"Ah! That is a good secret!" agreed Mole. "I'll give her a present."

"And come have tea with us," said Hare.

"Thank you, Hare," said Mole. "I don't think I need to tie you up again."

The three friends said good-bye and Grey Rabbit led the way through the wood to the great beech tree where Owl lived.

 Squirrel ran up the tree and called softly through the open window.

 "Wise Owl! Wise Owl! It's Grey Rabbit's birthday on Midsummer Day."

 "Gr-gr-gr-," snored Wise Owl, but he heard in his dreams all the same.

 They passed into the fields where Milkman Hedgehog was coming back from milking.

 "Can we have a drink?" asked Squirrel, dancing up to him. "It's thirsty work keeping secrets."

 Hare took Old Hedgehog aside and whispered to him:

 "It's Grey Rabbit's birthday on Midsummer Day. We are going to make her a cake, and you can come and taste it."

 "Ah! Thank you!" cried Hedgehog. "I'll make a present for Grey Rabbit."

 "Come along, Hare. We shall never get to the Speckledy Hen's house," called Grey Rabbit, "if you spend all the time telling secrets."

When they arrived at the farm, there was the Speckledy Hen out walking with her little parasol over her head.

"We've come for some eggs, Speckledy Hen," said Grey Rabbit. While the Hen was filling up the basket, Hare went and whispered in her ear.

"It's Grey Rabbit's birthday on Midsummer Day. We are going to make a cake and you can come and taste it."

"I'll bring a present for dear Grey Rabbit," whispered Hen. "And mind you put plenty of eggs in the cake, Hare."

The next day Squirrel and Hare decided to make the cake.

"We must get Grey Rabbit out of the way and do it secretly," said Hare. "Won't she be surprised! She doesn't know we can make cakes."

"We don't know either," muttered Squirrel. She was doubtful, but Hare was full of confidence.

"Grey Rabbit! Grey Rabbit! Go away! We don't want you!" commanded Hare sternly, when Grey Rabbit came in from the garden.

"Oh Hare! What have I done? What's the matter." Her ears drooped, and a tear came to her eye. Why was there such a mystery?

Squirrel stamped her foot.

"Hare! How stupid you are!" She wiped Grey Rabbit's eyes and then spoke kindly to her.

"Grey Rabbit! Will you please take a bottle of primrose wine to Wise Owl? Moldy Warp would like a visit, and I'm sure Fuzzypeg would love to hear a story."

"I'll run off at once," said Grey Rabbit, smiling at the two friends.

"Good-bye! Don't hurry back," called Squirrel and Hare, and they waved their paws as Grey Rabbit went along the lane.

"Quickly! Quickly!" cried Hare, and they bounded into the house.

Squirrel sprang onto the cupboard and sniffed at all the jars of spices and herbs.

"Here's tansy and woodruff, and preserved violets, and bottled cherries," said she.

"Here's fern seed and poppy seed, and acorns and beechnuts," said Hare. "Oh, here's the pepper pot. How much shall I put in?"

"A fistful of everything makes a nice cake," said Squirrel.

So they dipped their paws into every jar, and mixed the seeds and herbs in the yellow bowl.

"Is the oven hot?" said a deep voice, and they both sprang around in alarm. There, at the window, was Old Hedgehog watching them with twinkling eyes.

"I've come with extra milk for the cake," he said. "You shouldn't have forgotten the oven and you shouldn't have put pepper in the cake."

Hare blushed and tried to hide the pepper pot.

"Oh Hare! How could you! We shall have to begin all over again."

"I'll come and lend a hand," said Old Hedgehog. And he made up the fire and gave Hare the bellows to puff the flames. He showed Squirrel how to mix the sugar and butter together and how to sprinkle in the currants and spices.

Hare ran to the garden and brought in rose petals and violets and pinks and clover—all the sweet-smelling things he could find to add to the cake. He beat up the eggs till they were a yellow froth and Hedgehog dropped them into the mixture.

"Now I must be off," said Hedgehog. "Remember not to open the oven door till the good rich smell comes out."

They popped the cake in the oven and shut the door.

After a time there came a strong sweet smell which made Hare wrinkle his nose.

"The cake!" he cried. "It's telling us it's ready to come out."

So Squirrel wrapped a cloth around her paw and lifted out the good-smelling cake.

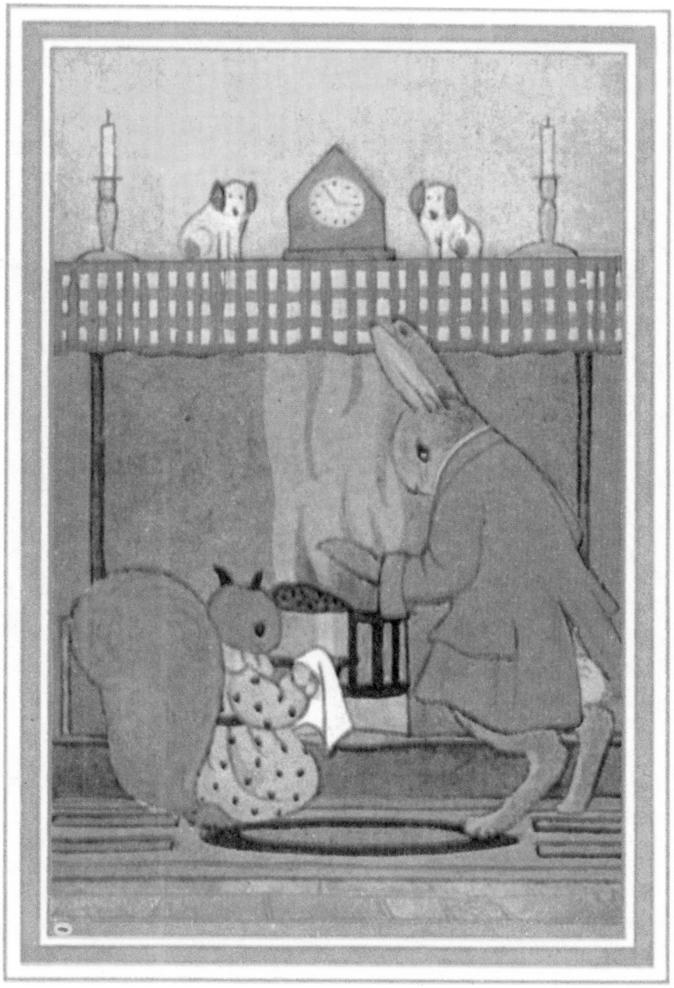

They carried it into the garden and hid it under
an empty beehive.

The next day when Grey Rabbit had gone out to
gather wool from the hedges, Squirrel ran to the
garden for the cake. She iced it and wrote GREY
RABBIT'S BIRTHDAY on the top in pollen dust.

Hare went to the cupboard and took out every
candle he could find. They put them all around the
edge and then they hid the cake in the beehive
again.

"I'm going to make a fan for Grey Rabbit," said
Squirrel. "I shall ask the green woodpecker and the
goldfinch for some feathers."

"And I will make a purse for her," said Hare.

Squirrel begged a few feathers from the birds.
She put them together, and there was the prettiest
little fan of green and gold.

Hare went to the pasture for a puffball. He squeezed out the dust, and washed the little bag in the dew, then he tied it with ribbon-grasses.

Darkness came and the three little animals went upstairs to bed. In the night Grey Rabbit was wakened by a faint noise under her window. She sat up and listened. Her eyes were wide open. She slipped out of bed and putting her cloak over her nightgown, she ran downstairs and into the garden. There, crouched in a sad, prickly little ball, was Fuzzypeg. "What's the matter, Fuzzypeg?" whispered Grey Rabbit.

"I came to say Happy Birthday," said Fuzzypeg. "I got out of the window, and I ran very fast, but I heard Wise Owl hooting, and I got frightened."

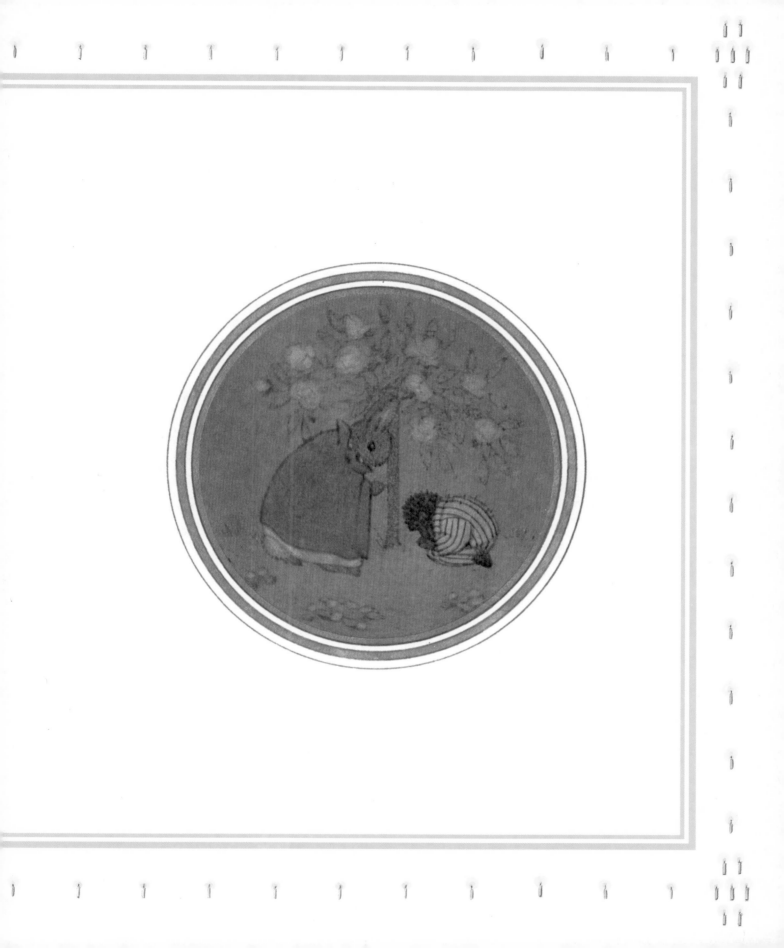

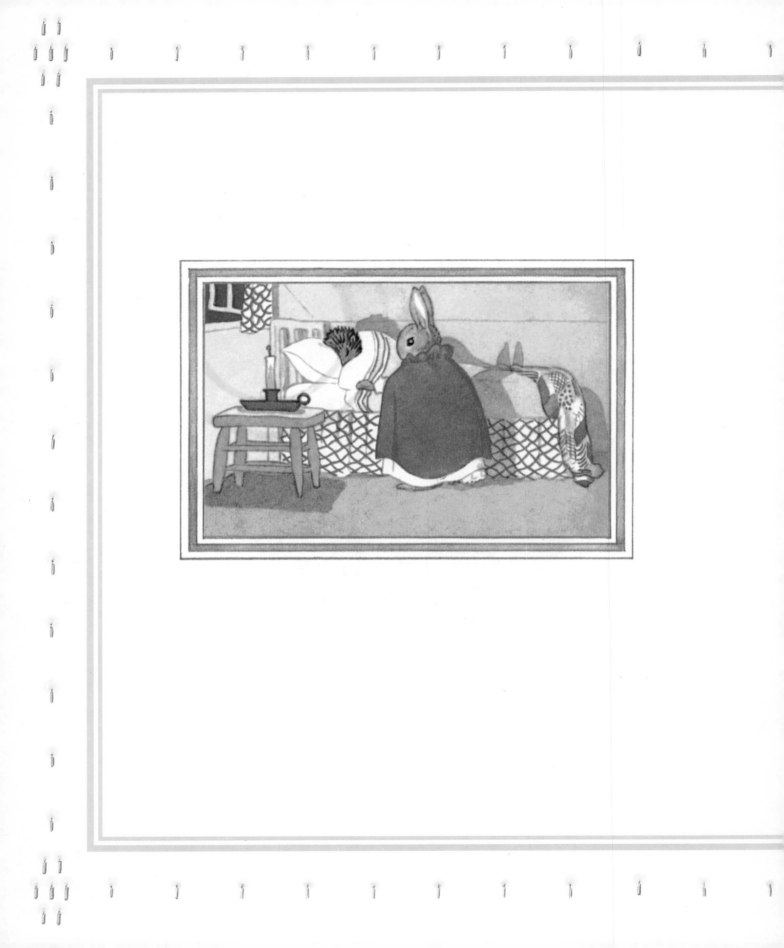

"Poor little Fuzzypeg," said Grey Rabbit softly. "You had better come into my bed." She took his paw and led him upstairs. He leaped into the pretty bed and looked around the room.

"Isn't it nice!" he cried. "I knew you'd take care of me, Grey Rabbit. Happy Birthday, Grey Rabbit."

"It isn't my birthday till tomorrow, Fuzzypeg," said Grey Rabbit.

She tucked him in, then she wrapped her cloak around herself and crept under the bed. She couldn't sleep with a bundle of prickles by her side.

"Grey Rabbit, is it tomorrow?" he called.

Far away they could hear the church clock strike midnight.

"Happy Birthday," said Fuzzypeg quickly.

The next morning Hare and Squirrel raced downstairs to get breakfast.

"I'm going to say Happy Birthday to Grey Rabbit," said Hare.

"So am I," said Squirrel.

So upstairs they bundled, and they flung open the bedroom door.

"Happy Birthday!" came squeaking from the bed.

"You don't say it, Grey Rabbit," said Hare. "We say it." He gave the bedclothes a hard pat.

Out of the blankets came Fuggypeg's dark head.

"Good morning," said he. "I said it first."

The noise wakened Grey Rabbit, and she crawled out from under the bed.

Hare and Squirrel were so surprised they never said "Happy Birthday" at all.

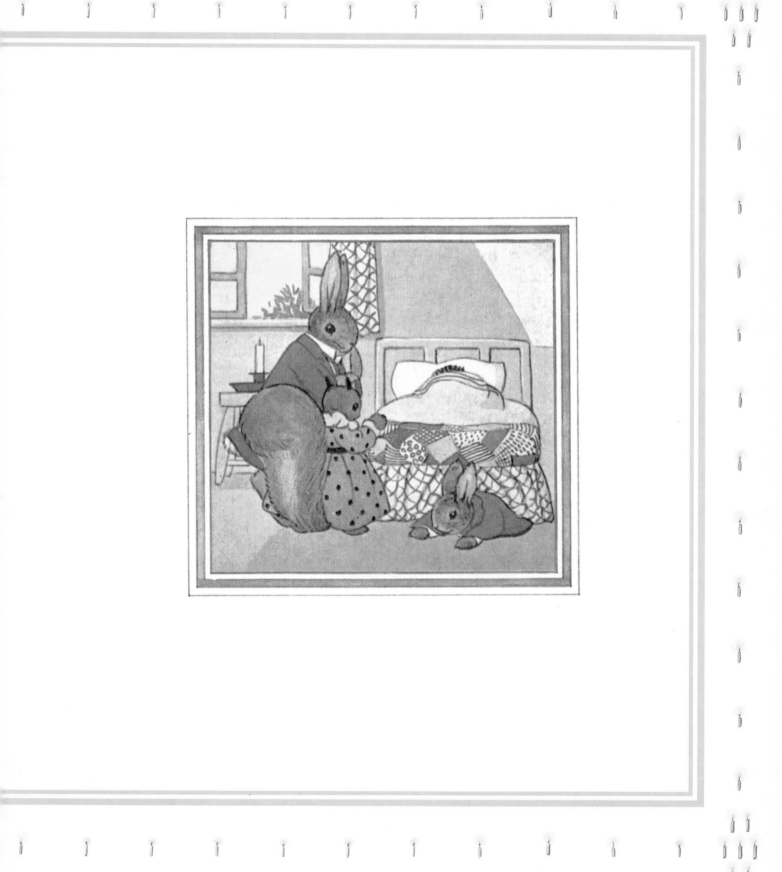

"Milk-o! Milk-o!" the call came from the kitchen. "Has anyone seen our Fuzzypeg? He ran away in the night, and it's my belief he came to see Miss Grey Rabbit."

"Here he is, Hedgehog!" they shouted, running downstairs.

"I said it first," boasted Fuzzypeg. "I said Happy Birthday before any of you."

"He said he would be the first, and he's done it," said Old Hedgehog proudly.

"Let him stay for breakfast," pleaded Grey Rabbit, and Hedgehog agreed. Fuzzypeg made some more toast and soon they were sitting around the table.

"It's your birthday, Grey Rabbit," said Squirrel, "so you shall have a holiday. We'll wash the cups and plates and make the beds."

"Then I'll go into the garden with Fuzzypeg and show him the flowers," said Grey Rabbit. When they came to the beehive a stream of honeybees flew out, and another stream flew in.

"Hare! Squirrel! Come here! A swarm of bees is living in our empty hive," called Grey Rabbit. "Isn't it exciting?"

"Oh! Oh! Oh!" cried Squirrel and Hare. "Oh! What shall we do?"

"Listen," said Grey Rabbit. "The bees are humming something," and this is what the animals heard:

"It's Grey Rabbit's Birthday,
She doesn't want money
Or fine clothes or riches.
We'll make her some honey."

Hare and Squirrel looked at one another and sighed.

At four o'clock they sent Grey Rabbit upstairs, while they got the tea ready. They ran into the garden to the beehive for the cake. Hare put a butterfly net over his head, lest he should be stung, but the bees had gone.

They lifted up the straw skep, and there was the cake, looking nicer than ever, and around it were many little pots of honey, each as big as a thimble. The pots were made of golden wax and the honey was scented with wild thyme.

They carried the treasures indoors and placed them on the table. Grey Rabbit came running downstairs.

"Oh! Oh!" cried Grey Rabbit. "What's this?"

"It's somebody's birthday cake," said Squirrel.

"It's everybody's cake, and here they come to the feast," said Hare.

Up the path came many little feet. Then there was a rat–tat–tat at the door.

"Come in! Come in!" cried Squirrel.

In trooped Moldy Warp, the Hedgehog family, Water Rat, the Speckledy Hen and a crowd of little animals.

"Many Happy Returns, Grey Rabbit," they cried. They saw the table, the lighted cake and the honey pots.

"Oh–oh–oh–oh! It's like Moldy Warp's Christmas tree."

Squirrel gave Grey Rabbit the little fan made of feathers. Hare brought out the purse tied with green ribbon-grass. Everybody had brought a present; but Moldy Warp's present was the best of all. It was the song of the nightingale in a tiny polished music box.

They were all listening to the music as Grey Rabbit turned the handle, when the door was pushed open and a round feathered head, and a pair of large blinking eyes appeared.

"I won't come in," hooted Wise Owl, "but I have brought a small token of my regard for Grey Rabbit."

He thrust one claw forward and dropped a book on the table. Then he drifted away as silently as he had come.

"Whew!" exclaimed Moldy Warp. "That was a shock."

"What has he brought?" asked Hare.

"It's called 'Wise Owl's Guide to Knowledge'," said Grey Rabbit, holding the tiny green volume.

"Cut the cake, Grey Rabbit!" called Hare. "I'm hungry. Cut the cake!"

So Grey Rabbit cut the beautiful birthday cake and they all had a piece. It was as good as it looked.

Moldy Warp drank to Grey Rabbit's health, and Water Rat made a speech. Squirrel recited a little poem and Hare played a tune on his flute.

They all laughed and sang and danced till night came, and then they went home by the light of the moon.

"What a lovely birthday it has been," said Grey Rabbit. "How kind everybody is to me."

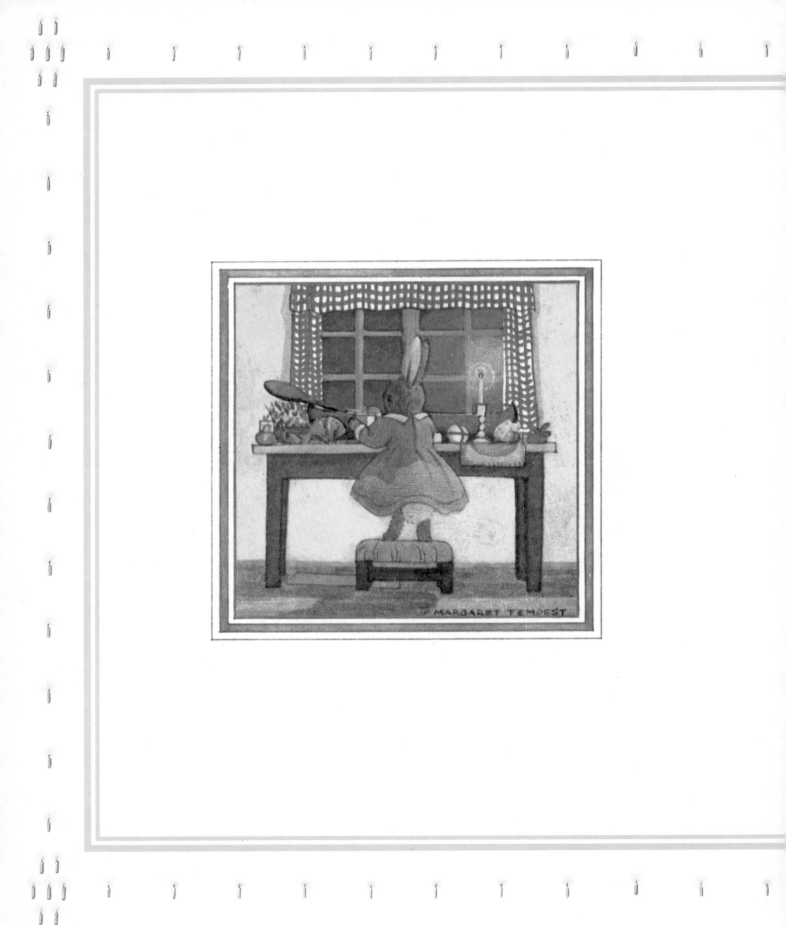

She looked at her presents on the table: the music box with the song of the nightingale, 'Wise Owl's Guide to Knowledge', a handkerchief from Mrs. Hedgehog, a tiny chestnut basket of flowers from Fuzzypeg, a little canoe from Water Rat, the feather fan, the puffball purse, the honey pots, and all the other little treasures.

She went upstairs to bed, with the music box under her arm. She turned the handle and the voice of the nightingale came trilling forth. From the woods another nightingale answered.

"Happy Birthday, Grey Rabbit," it seemed to say.

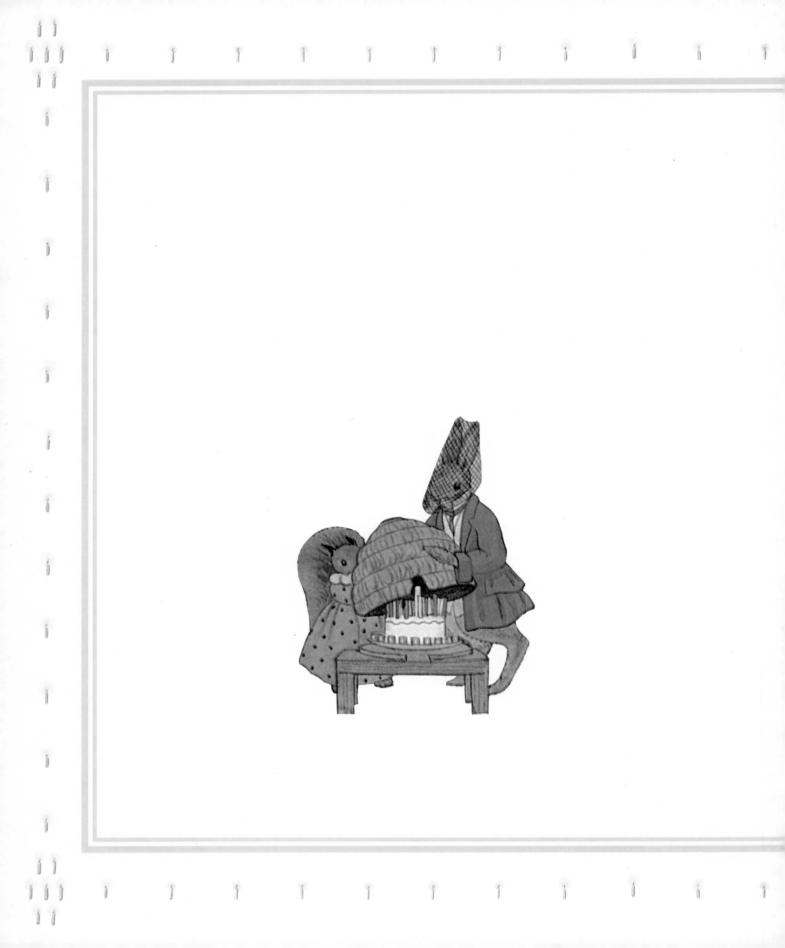